Enjoy this book!

Please remember to return it on time.
so that others may enjoy it too.

Manage your library account and
discover all we offer by visiting us
online at www.nashualibrary.org.

Love your library? Tell a friend!

Words Are Like Faces

By Edith Baer

Illustrated by Kyra Teis

STAR BRIGHT BOOKS

CAMBRIDGE, MASSACHUSETTS

Published in the United States of America by Star Bright Books, Inc. The name Star Bright Books and the Star
Bright Books logo are registered trademarks of Star Bright Books, Inc. Please visit www.starbrightbooks.com.
For bulk orders, please email: orders@starbrightbooks.com, or call customer service at: (617) 354-1300.

Previously published under ISBN 0-394-84028-3
Hardcover ISBN: 978-1-59572-108-2   Paperback ISBN: 978-1-59572-662-9
Star Bright Books / MA / 00208130   Star Bright Books / MA / 00108130
Printed in China / C&C / 9 8 7 6 5 4 3 2   Printed in China / C&C / 9 8 7 6 5 4 3 2 1

Library of Congress Cataloging-in-Publication Data

Baer, Edith.
  Words are like faces / by Edith Baer ; illustrated by Kyra Teis.
     p. cm.
  Summary: Rhyming text points out the many uses of words and the different emotions
and concepts they can convey.
  ISBN-13: 978-1-59572-108-2
  ISBN-10: 1-59572-108-8
 [1. Language and languages--Fiction. 2. Stories in rhyme.] I. Teis, Kyra, ill. II. Title.

PZ8.3.B137Wo 2007
[E]--dc22
                                          2006035881

To children everywhere,
     for the joy of words and reading.

—E. B.

For Jeff—heaven's way of smiling.

—K.T.

Words
can be

Spoken,

printed

or

Penned,

Put on a blackboard or mailed

to a friend

Passed as a secret
from one to another—
Words are what people
say to each other.

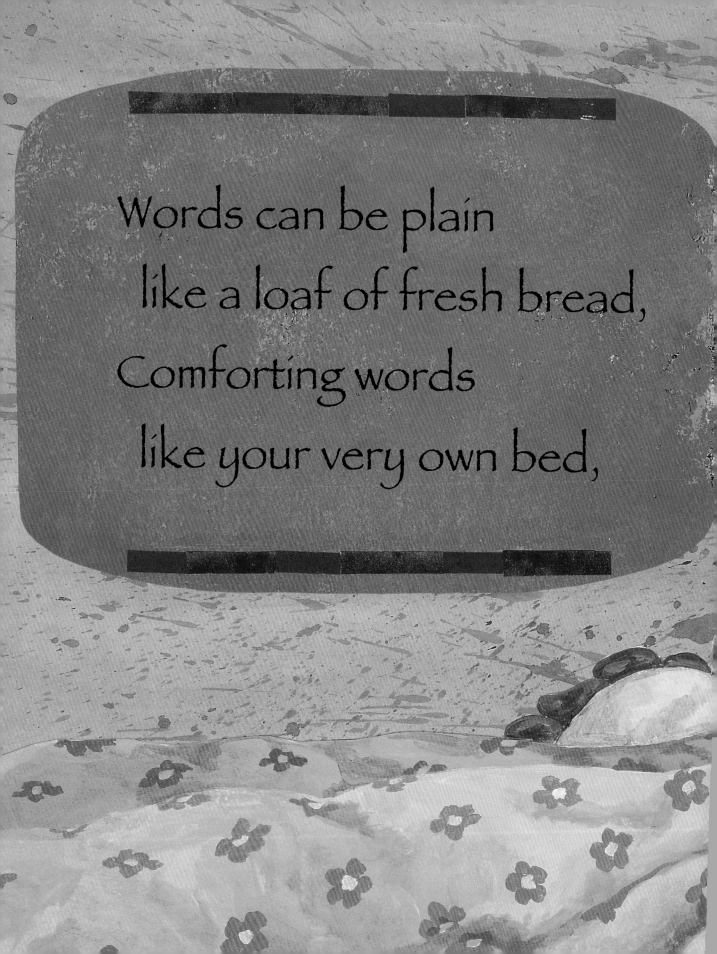

Words can be plain
like a loaf of fresh bread,
Comforting words
like your very own bed,

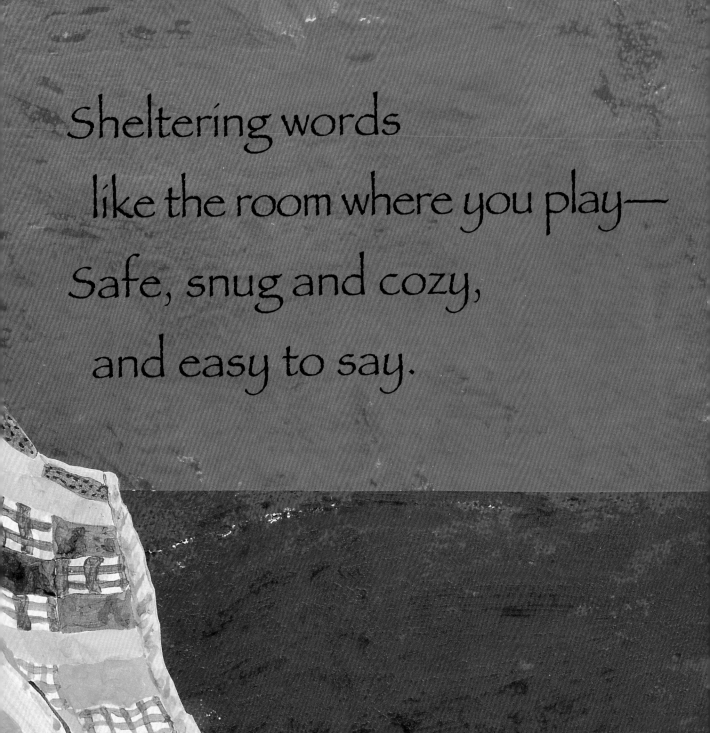

Sheltering words
   like the room where you play—
Safe, snug and cozy,
   and easy to say.

Words can be fleet things,

light as a cloud,

Lovely to hear

as you say them aloud—

Sunlight and rainbow,
snowflake and star—

They glimmer and shimmer
and shine from afar.

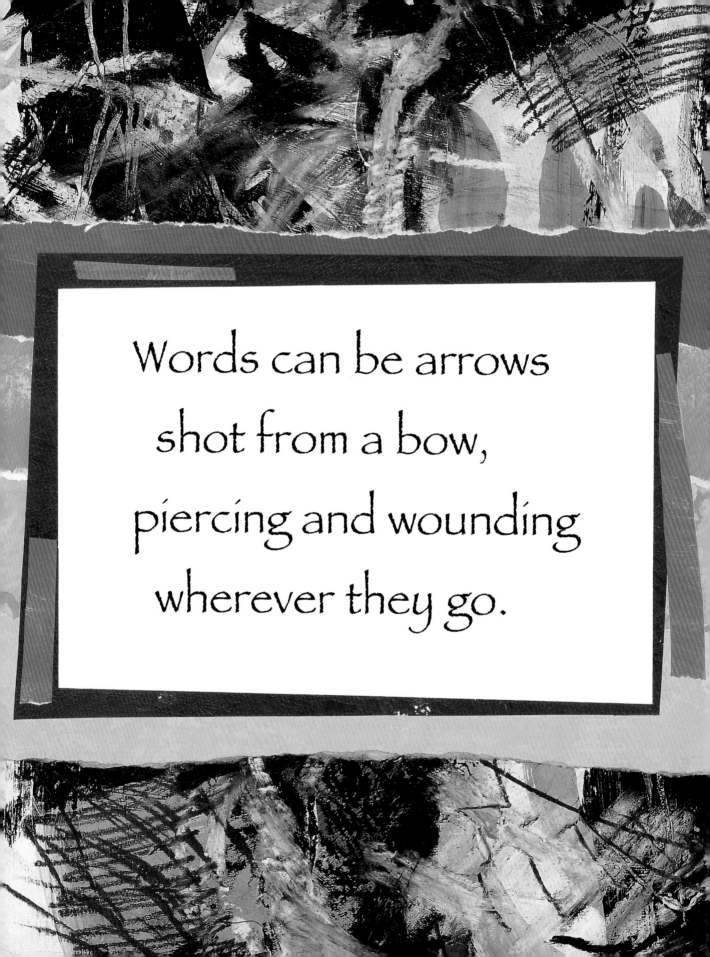

Words can be arrows shot from a bow, piercing and wounding wherever they go.

Words can be

soothing

and healing

instead.

Be careful
with words,

for they can't be unsaid.

Some words are like faces
we've known long before,
and some like new places
to find and explore.

Some

twirl on

tiptoes,

some

clatter

or clink,

and some sound exactly

the way you would think!

Do you have favorite
words of your own?
Milkshake or magic?
Old funny bone?

whippoorwill,

daffodil,

merry-go-round?

Touch them and taste them

and try on their sound!

Words say you're happy,
angry or sad,

make you feel better
when you feel bad,

get off your chest

what you're trying to hide—

Words tell what people

feel deep inside.

And remember. . .

Hurtful words spoken
can't be unsaid,
be careful with words
and choose kind ones instead.